ELIZABETH

Based on *The Railway Series* by the Rev. W. Awdry

Illustrations by
Robin Davies and Jerry Smith

EGMONT

EGMONT

we bring stories to life

First published in Great Britain in 2003
by Egmont UK Limited
239 Kensington High Street, London W8 6SA
This edition published in 2008

Thomas the Tank Engine & Friends™

CREATED BY BRITT ALLCROFT

Based on the Railway Series by the Reverend W Awdry
© 2008 Gullane (Thomas) LLC. A HIT Entertainment company.
Thomas the Tank Engine & Friends and Thomas & Friends are trademarks of Gullane (Thomas) Limited.
Thomas the Tank Engine & Friends and Design is Reg. U.S. Pat. & Tm. Off

HiT entertainment

ISBN 978 1 4052 3452 8
1 3 5 7 9 10 8 6 4 2
Printed in Italy

The Forest Stewardship Council (FSC) is an international, non-governmental organisation dedicated to promoting responsible management of the world's forests. FSC operates a system of forest certification and product labelling that allows consumers to identify wood and wood-based products from well managed forests.

For more information about Egmont's paper buying policy please visit www.egmont.co.uk/ethicalpublishing

For more information about the FSC please visit their website at www.fsc.uk.org

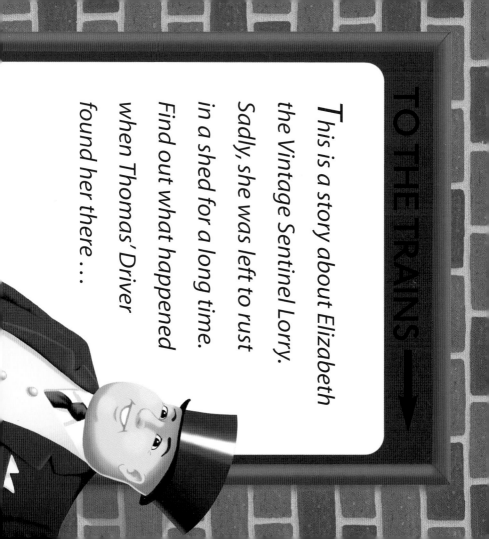

TO THE TRAINS →

This is a story about Elizabeth
the Vintage Sentinel Lorry.
Sadly, she was left to rust
in a shed for a long time.
Find out what happened
when Thomas' Driver
found her there . . .

Thomas was taking heavy goods trucks to a cargo ship at Brendam Docks. The ship was leaving at sundown, so Thomas had to work hard to get the trucks there in time.

Suddenly, one of his coupling rods broke.

His Driver saw a shed by the track.

"I'll see if there are some tools in there," he said.

"Be careful! That shed looks a bit spooky," said Thomas.

Then a voice came from inside the shed:

"Be quiet out there, I'm trying to sleep!"

Thomas' Driver went into the shed. After a few moments, he came out again.

"Well? Is it a ghost?" asked Thomas.

"No!" laughed his Driver, "It's not a ghost. It's a very helpful surprise."

Thomas' Driver and Fireman took coal into the shed. Thomas wondered what they were doing.

"She should be able to get us to the fitter's yard," Thomas heard his Driver say.

"If her boiler holds," replied his Fireman.

"She badly needs repair work."

Thomas heard lots of clanking noises coming from the shed. What could be inside?

At last, out of the shed drove a rather dirty, old steam lorry.

"Thomas, this is Elizabeth," said his Driver.

"So you're the little puffer that has broken down," said Elizabeth to Thomas.

Thomas didn't like that at all. "You're a rude, old steam lorry!" he replied, sharply.

"Actually, I'm a Vintage Sentinel Lorry," replied Elizabeth. "And you should be thankful that I'm here to help you!"

Elizabeth and Thomas' Driver went to the fitter's yard. Elizabeth's engine made loud grinding noises. As she drove up a steep hill, her engine got louder and louder.

"You're not built for hills," said Thomas' Driver. "Will you make it?"

"I'll be fine," replied Elizabeth. "I'm just catching my breath."

Before long, Elizabeth reached the fitter's yard. Thomas' Driver fetched a new coupling rod and they drove back to Thomas.

Elizabeth felt very proud. She realised she had been in the shed for so long that she had forgotten how much fun it was to help others.

Thomas was impressed with how quickly Elizabeth had fetched the coupling rod.

He was about to thank her, when she said, "Next time, make sure you're not so careless!"

Now Thomas thought Elizabeth was the rudest lorry he had ever met! He waited in silence while his Driver fitted the new coupling rod, then he set off to the Docks.

Elizabeth decided to follow Thomas to the Docks. "That little puffer has already broken one coupling rod, so he may well need my help again!" she thought.

Elizabeth's engine rattled and groaned as she slowly followed behind Thomas. Soon Thomas was out of sight, but Elizabeth didn't mind. She remembered which roads she had to take to get to the Docks.

Thomas arrived at the Docks just in time. As the goods were unloaded from his trucks, The Fat Controller came over. He looked very cross indeed.

"Where have you been?" he asked. "You nearly missed the boat!"

Thomas told him about his broken coupling rod. He was about to tell him about Elizabeth, when she drove up!

"Oh! It's you!" said Elizabeth to The Fat Controller. "Have you learnt how to drive properly yet?"

Thomas thought The Fat Controller would be very angry, but to his surprise The Fat Controller said, "Elizabeth! The first lorry I ever drove. How marvellous to see you again! Where have you been?"

Thomas couldn't believe it – Elizabeth and The Fat Controller were friends!

Elizabeth told The Fat Controller that she had been left in the shed a long time ago and everyone had forgotten about her. She had thought she would never drive again.

The Fat Controller was really pleased that Elizabeth had been found. He asked Jem Cole, the mechanic, to restore her to her original beauty. Elizabeth smiled happily and thanked The Fat Controller. She could hardly wait to be in full working order again.

A few weeks later, Elizabeth drove past The Fat Controller's station. Her paintwork shone and her engine sounded perfect.

"Hello," she said. "Don't you think my new paintwork looks marvellous?"

"You're the grandest lorry in the whole railroad!" replied The Fat Controller.

Thomas had to agree. And Elizabeth was so happy now she was useful again, that she wasn't rude at all!

The Thomas Story Library is THE definitive collection of stories about Thomas and ALL his friends.

5 more Thomas Story Library titles will be chuffing into your local bookshop in August 2008!

Jeremy

Hector

BoCo

Billy

Whiff

And there are even more Thomas Story Library books to follow late

So go on, start your Thomas Story Library NOW!

A Fantastic Offer for Thomas the Tank Engine Fans!

In every Thomas Story Library book like this one, you will find a special token. Collect 6 Thomas tokens and we will send you a brilliant Thomas poster, and a double-sided bedroom door hanger! Simply tape a £1 coin in the space above, and fill out the form overleaf.

STICK POUND COIN HERE

THOMAS TOKEN • 1 THOMAS TOKEN • 1 THOMAS

cut along the dotted line

TO BE COMPLETED BY AN ADULT

To apply for this great offer, ask an adult to complete the coupon below and send it with a pound coin and 6 tokens, to:
THOMAS OFFERS, PO BOX 715, HORSHAM RH12 5WG

☐ Please send a Thomas poster and door hanger. I enclose 6 tokens plus a £1 coin. (Price includes P&P)

Fan's name...

Address...

....Postcode...........

Date of birth...

Name of parent/guardian...

Signature of parent/guardian......................................

Please allow 28 days for delivery. Offer is only available while stocks last. We reserve the right to change the terms of this offer at any time and we offer a 14 day money back guarantee. This does not affect your statutory rights.

☐ Data Protection Act: If you do not wish to receive other similar offers from us or companies we recommend, please tick this box. Offers apply to UK only.